Adapted by Jasmine Jones
Based on the series created by Terri Minsky
Part One is based on a teleplay written
by Bob Thomas.
Part Two is based on a teleplay written
by Douglas Tuber and Tim Maile.

EGMONT

MORE LIZZIE BOOKS TO CHECK OUT!

WHEN MOMS ATTACK!

TOTALLY CRUSHED!

LIZZIE GOES WILD

THE RISE AND FALL OF THE KATE EMPIRE

PICTURE THIS

NEW KID IN SCHOOL

BROKEN HEARTS

JUST LIKE LIZZIE

LIZZIE LOVES ETHAN

STRAPPED FOR CASH

HEAD OVER HEELS

MY QUIZ BOOK
More than 20 quizzes about boys, school,
friends – and Lizzie!

DON'T EVEN GO THERE!
A little book of Lizzie-isms

Lizzie McGuire

PART
ONE

First published in the USA 2003 by Disney Press
Published in Great Britain 2004
by Egmont Books Limited
239 Kensington High Street, London W8 6SA

Published by arrangement with Disney Press,
114 Fifth Avenue, New York, New York 10011-5690

ISBN 1 4052 1426 0

1 3 5 7 9 10 8 6 4 2

A CIP catalogue record for this title is available
from the British Library

Printed and bound in the UK

CHAPTER ONE

"I saw the grossest thing this morning," Lizzie McGuire said as she walked toward homeroom with her best friends, David "Gordo" Gordon and Miranda Sanchez. "And it was floating," Lizzie added. She shuddered at the memory. The truth was, she wasn't one hundred percent sure what the thing was, although she had a few ideas—all repulsive. Lizzie definitely knew something gross when she saw it. She did, after all, have a little brother, and Matt McGuire was pretty much

1

the master of revolting stuff.

"In the air?" Gordo asked, seemingly intrigued by the unnamed floating grossness.

Miranda curled her lip at him and blinked. Gordo was a good friend, but he could be kind of peculiar.

"No, no," Lizzie said. She jerked her head toward the exit doors. "In the water fountain outside the school," she explained. The three friends walked into class and plopped into their chairs.

Miranda grimaced. "I don't want to hear about this."

"I do," Gordo said eagerly.

Miranda groaned as a shriek of feedback blasted out from the loudspeakers. Lizzie plugged her ears. The annoying (not to mention, painful!) sound lasted a few moments before the voice of the equally annoying, nerdiest kid in the universe—Larry

Tudgeman—came over the loudspeaker.

"Good morning," Larry said brightly. "Lawrence Tudgeman the third here with your morning announcements."

"So, what exactly was floating in the water fountain?" Gordo whispered as he leaned toward Lizzie.

Lizzie made a sour face. How could she possibly describe the gross thing she had seen? It was beyond description.

"So, whoever put the . . . *you-know-what* in the water fountain this morning," Larry droned over the PA system, "the principal's going to find out who you are . . . *Joey.*"

Lizzie rolled her eyes. Was Larry Tudgeman insane? Joey Wannamaker is the biggest bully in the school, she thought. And she meant "biggest" literally. The rumor was that Joey had actually flunked seventh grade eight times. And he certainly looked more like a college sophomore than a junior high school student. Not that he looked as smart or mature or anything—he was just . . . big!

"I mean, not that I would tell anybody, *Joey* . . ." Larry's voice droned on over the loudspeaker, "so let's just forget that I ever said it, okay, *Joey* . . . ?"

Lizzie rolled her eyes. She could just picture Larry wearing that know-it-all smile of his as he sat behind the microphone.

"I would not want to be Joey," Miranda said.

Gordo lifted an eyebrow. "I would not want to be *Tudgeman*."

Good point, Lizzie thought.

"Anyway . . ." Larry went on, switching into his official "news announcement" voice, "next Monday we will be voting on class favorites."

Gordo snorted. "Great. Yet another opportunity to make students feel inadequate." He shook his head.

Larry continued. "The categories are Best Looking—"

Lizzie looked at the ceiling and sighed. "Cheerleader," she said. Miranda flashed her a look that said "of course".

"—Best Dressed—" Larry said.

Miranda twirled her hair and rolled her eyes. "Cheerleader," she said in a mock perky voice.

"Most Poised," Larry went on, "and Most Likely to Succeed. Hi, Joey."

Suddenly, there was another shriek of feedback. Then, several loud *thunks* barked from the loudspeaker.

Gordo sat back in his chair and shuddered at the noise. "I guess the announcements are over," he said.

Something is definitely over, Lizzie thought.

She just hoped that it wasn't Larry's life.

Just then, the bell rang. Lizzie hauled herself out of her seat toward her first-period class.

"So, who do you think will win Best Looking?" Miranda asked as she slung her book bag over her shoulder.

Lizzie shrugged. There were really only two possibilities. "Kate or Claire," Lizzie said, naming the two snobbiest and most popular girls in the school. They were the ultimate queen bees . . . and both were cheerleaders, of course.

Miranda nodded. "What about Best Dressed?"

Lizzie scoffed, again thinking about the only two possible candidates. "Whoever doesn't win Best Looking."

Miranda pressed her lips together. "How about Most Poised?" she asked.

"Hey!" Lizzie said brightly, seeing a chink

in the cheerleader armor. "I could win that one."

Gordo cocked an eyebrow. "Poised?" he said, pointing dubiously toward Lizzie. "Balanced? Easy manner? Graceful?"

Lizzie frowned at Gordo. Okay, it was true—there had been one or two times when she had opened her locker into her own face. And she guessed that she *had* tripped over her share of library carts that had been left carelessly in the middle of the hallway. But that didn't mean that she wasn't poised, did it?

"Okay," Lizzie finally admitted after thinking it over briefly. "Maybe not." Still, she thought, that prize has to go to someone besides Kate or Claire. Someone with style. Someone who doesn't fall down a lot. Someone like . . . Lizzie thought hard. "That sounds more like you, Miranda."

Miranda's eyebrows disappeared beneath

the straight black line of her bangs. "You think?" She seemed really surprised by the idea.

"Yeah," Lizzie said quickly. "I mean, you haven't tripped, fallen, or spilled anything on yourself the whole entire year. . . ."

"Neither have I," Gordo pointed out.

Lizzie looked at him with half-closed eyes. Had Gordo completely forgotten the time he'd built the giant brain for science class that overloaded and exploded all over . . . well, all over *everything*?

". . . Or blown up any science experiments," she added.

"That was a long time ago," Gordo said.

"People remember," Lizzie insisted. Believe me, she thought, an exploding brain is a difficult thing to forget. I've tried.

"Fine," Gordo huffed. "Then I'm going for

Most Photographed This Year."

Lizzie frowned. "Is that even a category?"

"When the yearbook first comes out, what's the thing that everyone does?" Gordo demanded.

"Draw a mustache on Coach Kelly's picture?" Miranda suggested. Coach Kelly was the torturous gym teacher who actually considered square dancing a sport. She deserved that mustache.

Gordo shook his head. "No, no," he insisted. "After that, they all count how many times they got their picture in it."

Lizzie thought about this for a moment. It was true. In fact, she usually went through the yearbook with a magnifying glass, just to make sure she hadn't missed any pictures of herself.

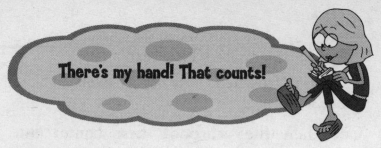

There's my hand! That counts!

Geez, how embarrassing. "I don't do that," Lizzie fibbed.

Gordo looked at her doubtfully. "How many times were you in the last yearbook?" he asked dryly.

"Three," Lizzie said automatically. Doh! Now she had given herself away. "I think it was three," she added slowly, as though she couldn't quite remember. She fiddled with her hair.

Gordo looked over at Miranda, who was doing the very same hair-fiddling thing as Lizzie, pretending she had no idea how many times her picture was in the yearbook. Gordo lifted his eyebrows in suspicious disbelief.

Miranda sighed. "Five," she admitted finally.

Lizzie smiled. Busted. Gordo was right, as usual.

"See?" Gordo asked. "Everybody keeps 'the Count'. So this year, I'm going to set a record. I'm going to be . . . *everywhere*." He shook his head and added in his best Elvis Presley voice, "Thank you very much."

Lizzie laughed. Leave it to Gordo to come up with his own class-favorite category. And she had no doubt that he'd win it, too.

"Well, I definitely think that you are Most Poised material," Lizzie said to Miranda later that day. Lizzie was shuffling through her locker, looking for her history notebook.

Miranda shrugged. "I don't really feel like 'Most' anything," she admitted.

"That's what Kate wants you to think," Gordo said, waving his hand dismissively. "That way you never even try. It's her way of maintaining the status quo."

Lizzie screwed up her face and frowned at Gordo. Couldn't he just speak English, like a normal person? "Status quo?" Lizzie repeated.

"It means that Kate wants to keep things the way they are," Gordo explained.

Miranda scowled at him. "Why didn't you just say that?" she snapped. Miranda had even less patience with Gordo's vocabulary than Lizzie did.

"Uh, I did," Gordo replied.

"Well, I say no more quo," Lizzie said quickly. "If someone completely normal came to school on voting day dressed in an outrageously hip outfit, well, then they'd get the vote."

Gordo looked at her and nodded. "So—" he said, "—do it."

Lizzie blinked at him in surprise. "Me?" Why did Gordo have to pick today to take one of my suggestions seriously? she wondered.

"All you have to do is be better dressed than Kate or Claire for this one day," Gordo went on, like it would be the easiest thing in the world to outdress the coolest, hippest, most fabulous fashionistas to ever walk into their school.

But even Miranda was going along with the impossible dream. "And win Best Dressed," she added, smiling at Lizzie eagerly. "You can break the status cow!"

"Quo," Gordo corrected.

Miranda sighed impatiently. "Whatever," she snapped.

"I wouldn't know what to wear," Lizzie said uncertainly. She glanced down at her outfit—pink velour pants, belt with sparkly buckle, and pink and white tee: cute, but definitely not something that would set the fashion world on fire.

"There's a hot new pair of hip-huggers in the window at the Style Shack!" Miranda gushed. "All the music video people get clothes there. Kate and Claire might as well not even show up." Miranda smiled smugly.

"All you have to do is outdress Kate and Claire for one day," Gordo repeated, "and you'll be Best Dressed in the yearbook . . . forever."

Lizzie bit her lip. "Forever?"

Miranda lifted her eyebrows and nodded.

"Forever," Gordo replied.

Lizzie thought about that. Best Dressed . . . forever.

She just had to find a way to make this work!

CHAPTER TWO

"Hey, Mom—there you are," Lizzie said as she walked into the kitchen. Mrs. McGuire didn't look up—she was too engrossed in funneling a gigantic barrel of yellow mustard into a small squeeze bottle. Lizzie eyed the small bottle. That was so like her mother—to buy a little container of the good stuff and fill it up with the generic brand. But Lizzie didn't have time to think about that right now. She had to put her plan to be Best Dressed Forever into motion. She decided not to beat around the bush.

"Hey, listen, Monday is yearbook voting and I was hoping to maybe make Best Dressed," she said to her mom.

Mrs. McGuire put the gigantic mustard barrel down and looked at Lizzie over the top of her rectangular glasses. "Best Dressed?" She snorted. "Are they still voting on that? It's so materialistic." She shook her head and sighed, adjusting her mustard funnel. Then, she suddenly put it down. "It would be cool if you won, though. Huh?" She smiled warmly at the thought.

Lizzie giggled. "Exactly," she said, flashing her mom a bright grin.

"I remember when I was your age," Lizzie's mom said. "Coco Newbury always won Best Dressed."

Mrs. McGuire's gaze drifted off, and Lizzie knew that her mom was picturing Coco in all of her fabulous late-seventies glory—some kind of brown prairie skirt and brown macramé top, no doubt.

"Well, listen," Mrs. McGuire said suddenly, snapping back to reality, "you, uh, you want me to help you with anything? You need anything washed or ironed?"

"Actually," Lizzie hedged, "there's this really cool pair of hip-huggers at the Style Shack, and this awesome top. . . ."

Mrs. McGuire lifted her eyebrows. "Well, how much?" she asked patiently. "Tell me."

"Oh." Lizzie winced and looked at her mom hopefully. "A hundred and ten dollars."

Mrs. McGuire gasped. "A hundred and ten . . ." she repeated, gaping at her daughter. "Honey, this household runs on a budget."

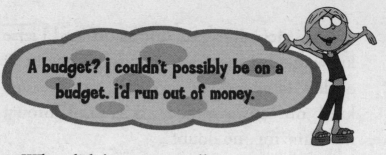

A budget? I couldn't possibly be on a budget. I'd run out of money.

Why didn't anyone tell me we were on a budget? Lizzie wondered. I just thought that Mom and Dad were kind of stingy . . . and that I hadn't gotten a raise in my allowance because my room was a mess.

But that wasn't the same thing as a budget. A budget meant that their house ran on a limited amount of money. Lizzie had just assumed that she could get more whenever she needed a refill.

"But, Mom," Lizzie protested. "This is an emergency . . . a clothes emergency."

"Well, I hate to be the bearer of bad news," Lizzie's mom said, "but the money tree in the backyard died."

Lizzie rolled her eyes. She hated it when her mom tried to be sarcastic. It always ended up sounding lame.

"But I thought you wanted to help me win," Lizzie protested.

"Well, I want to," Mrs. McGuire said as she put away her humongous tub of mustard, "but this house still runs on a budget. I mean, we just put new brake shoes on the car."

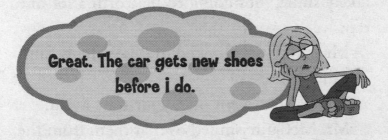

Great. The car gets new shoes before i do.

Lizzie sighed in frustration. This was going nowhere.

Just then, Lizzie's little brother, Matt, walked into the kitchen, followed by their dad. Matt walked right up to the fridge. But instead of yanking it open and chugging the root beer straight from the two-liter bottle and then complaining that they were out of string cheese and jerky the way he usually did, he pulled out a pen and signed his class picture, which was stuck to the fridge door with a magnet. Then he whipped the photo off the fridge and handed it to Mrs. McGuire.

"Better not lose that," Matt said with a cocky smile. "It's going to be worth a lot one day."

Mrs. McGuire looked at Matt doubtfully. "Really?"

"Yep," Matt went on, "your son's a star."

Mr. McGuire smiled over at them from the far end of the kitchen island, where he was busy polishing a green apple against his shirt. He was wearing a baseball cap and a jersey with green sleeves. He and Matt must have just gone to one of those minor league games they loved so much. Mr. McGuire always wore that getup to those games.

Mrs. McGuire looked confused. "Are they still running that Cardio Punch ad?" she asked her husband as she shut the fridge.

Lizzie bit her lip to keep from snorting. Her little brother had been the star of the lamest ad in the history of the world. Of course, the company had aired it about eight zillion times, and sent Matt a couple of huge checks that Mrs. McGuire had deposited into CDs. Matt had been really psyched about the CDs, and Lizzie had been really jealous . . . until their parents explained that these weren't the kind that you listen to, but the kind you invest money in.

"*The Uncle Wendell Show* was taping at the ballpark," Mr. McGuire explained. "Matt made this crazy face and cracked everybody up."

Lizzie almost spontaneously blurted out that

Matt's normal face cracks people up, but held back. After all, she was trying to stay on her mom's good side . . . just in case there was any money to be had. Still, Lizzie couldn't resist one little comment. She didn't want Matt to get an even bigger head than he already had.

"The Uncle Wendell Show?" she asked. "I think I watched that when I was still in diapers."

"So, you're still watching it?" Matt asked, blinking at her innocently.

Lizzie flashed her brother a huge, fake smile, and glared at him at the same time.

"They asked us to bring Matt back next week," Mr. McGuire went on, ignoring the little family feud going on around him.

"And every week," Matt added. "They said I had pizzazz."

"I'm sure they did," Lizzie snapped, "because I can smell it from here."

"Mom!" Matt wailed.

Lizzie stared at the ceiling and sighed. Typical Matt—he could dish it out, but he couldn't take it. Especially when it was a really good one. Lizzie's mom gave her a playful swat on the arm.

"Now, now," Mr. McGuire said patiently. "My son, the TV star."

"My brother, the *Uncle Wendell* dork," Lizzie added.

"Lizzie," Mrs. McGuire warned, frowning.

"Mom, I mean *dork* in a very loving way," Lizzie protested. She turned to leave, but Mrs. McGuire placed a gentle hand on her arm.

"Listen," her mom said gently, "what do you say you and I go through your closet and try to put together a few new outfits?"

Lizzie sighed. She knew that her mom was trying to be helpful . . . but it just wasn't working. "Mom, everybody at school has already seen my clothes." Lizzie shook her head. "You lost to Coco, and I'm going to lose to Kate." Lizzie blinked rapidly to clear the tears from her eyes. So close. She had come so close to being a best *something*. And now she was just going to be a best *nothing*. Lizzie hurried out of the kitchen before her mom could make it worse by saying how sorry she was.

"Coco?" Lizzie's dad said as he bit into his apple. "I remember Coco. She was hot."

"She was not hot," Mrs. McGuire protested. "She was just well dressed."

Matt stood at the color printer, staring at printouts of his own goofy face, which came spooling out over and over. "Four hundred ninety-eight . . ." he counted as another picture landed on the top of the huge stack in the printer tray. "Four hundred ninety-nine . . . five hundred . . ."

"Good morning, sweetie," Mrs. McGuire said sleepily as she wandered into the kitchen.

"Morning," Matt said absently as he continued to watch his pictures pile up.

Mrs. McGuire smiled at the printer, which was humming away. "What are you doing?"

"Making copies of my picture," Matt replied. "Let's see . . . five hundred six . . . five hundred seven . . ."

The smile dropped from Mrs. McGuire's face. "Five hundred?" she repeated.

"Five hundred one . . ." Matt said, "five hundred two . . ." He stopped suddenly, unsure whether he had already counted five hundred two. Oh, well. It was about five hundred. If there weren't enough, the fans would have to make do.

"Five hundred?" Mrs. McGuire repeated.

"Five hundred one . . ." Matt said again.

The printer beeped.

"Mom, we're out of paper," Matt informed her.

"We're out of paper?" Mrs. McGuire repeated. She stared at Matt. "You used all the paper making copies of your picture?"

"They're not for me," Matt protested. "They're for my fans."

"Morning, Mom," Lizzie said as she shuffled into the kitchen.

"Morning, sweetheart . . ." Mrs. McGuire said. Then she and Lizzie spoke at the same time. "I . . ."

Lizzie and her mom smiled at each other. Lizzie waved for her mom to continue.

"I just wanted to say that I was up all night tossing and turning." Mrs. McGuire grinned. "But I think that I have worked it all out."

Lizzie blinked. Was her mom really saying what Lizzie thought she was saying? That the jeans from the Style Shack were hers? That she was going to be Best Dressed . . . Forever? "That's, that's terrific, Mom!" Lizzie gasped. She could hardly wait to call Miranda! Lizzie was smiling so hard that her face was actually starting to hurt.

"Great!" Mrs. McGuire said happily. "So, I would like to take you bargain hunting on Saturday."

"Bargain hunting?" Lizzie's smile vanished, and she raised her eyebrows. Oh, no. No, no, no, no, no. This was not what I wanted to hear, Lizzie thought. I wanted to hear that I was going to the Style Shack—not the bargain basement! Shacks don't even *have* basements! Lizzie pictured herself strutting into school in an outfit made up of clothes that all of the stylish people who wore stylish clothes in stylish sizes had already passed up. If her mom thought that there was any way Lizzie could possibly win Best Dressed in some kind of polka-dot outfit in size Extra-Extra Large, Mrs. McGuire must have been sniffing the barrel of generic brand mustard instead of just using it to fool her family into thinking that they always used the good brand.

Mrs. McGuire smiled hopefully at Lizzie. It was obvious that she really, truly thought that this was the greatest idea since Velcro. Lizzie just couldn't bear to burst her mom's bubble. "Great," Lizzie said weakly.

it's called Style Shack for a reason. I'm not going to be voted Best Dressed wearing last year's rejects from a bargain basement.

But it looked like Lizzie had no choice.

Maybe I can just wear the unicorn sweater that Gammy McGuire sent me, instead, Lizzie thought miserably as she remembered the hideous outfit that her mom made her wear to school on picture day. If I'm going to have to wear something lame to school, I might as well go with what I've already got.

CHAPTER THREE

Matt grinned as he walked toward his locker. He hadn't given away any of his photographs yet . . . but he was sure that they would go like hotcakes once people started to recognize him. He banged on his orange locker door, but it didn't budge. That was odd. It usually only took one whack to get the thing open. Matt pounded on the locker.

"Excuse me."

Matt stopped banging and turned to see a

little girl from the first grade. She looked up at Matt with big brown eyes. "Are you that goofy-face kid from *The Uncle Wendell Show*?" she asked earnestly.

"Why, yes," Matt said. "Yes, I am."

"Can I have your autograph?" the little girl asked.

"Why, yes. Yes, you can." Matt pulled one of his photos out of his book bag and motioned for the girl to turn her back to him. "Turn around," he said as he drew a pen from his pocket. He leaned the paper on the girl's back and he signed the photo with a flourish. "Here you go," he said, handing over the photo.

"Thanks," the girl said, beaming at the autograph.

Matt smiled as he watched her walk away. "And so it begins," he murmured. Ah, stardom. It was even better than he had thought it would be.

* * *

Lizzie walked out onto the lunch patio and spotted Gordo contemplating a large map, which was laid out in front of him like a tablecloth. This was something new.

"So, where are the pants from the Smiley Shack?" Gordo asked as Lizzie walked over to join him.

"Actually, it's Style Shack. . . ." Lizzie corrected. Gordo was not exactly a fashion maven—he had no clue about style—shacks or otherwise. "And they're still being worn by the world's best-dressed mannequin." Lizzie frowned down at the map. "What's that?" she asked.

"Oh, this? This is a map of the school." Gordo pointed to the folded piece of notebook paper in his hand. "But this . . . this is a list of where the photographer will be at all times next week. Wherever he is, you'll find me." Gordo grinned evilly. Well, evilly for Gordo at least.

Just then, Miranda walked onto the patio. There was something new about her stride—her back was perfectly straight, her chin was up, and she almost seemed to glide as she made her way over to where her friends were sitting.

"Wow," Lizzie said, "I never realized Miranda was . . . so . . . poised."

Miranda slid gracefully into a seat. "Hey, guys," she said. "Catch this. I've had people come up to me and tell me they're going to vote for me as Most Poised. Me . . . maybe a Most!" She grinned.

"This is so exciting!" Lizzie cried. "My best friend Most Poised and Gordo is going to be Most Photographed."

Miranda giggled. "And after we go to the mall this Saturday," Miranda said, gesturing as though she could see Lizzie's name in lights, "Lizzie McGuire . . . Best Dressed."

Lizzie winced. "Actually, no mall. My mom has decided to take me"—Lizzie shuddered—"bargain hunting."

Miranda's jaw dropped. "Bargain hunting?" She said it in the same voice she might have used to say "sewer swimming?" "Is she serious?" Miranda asked. "How are you supposed to outdress Kate and Claire with, with . . . bargains?" She spat the last word like it was something gross that she had accidentally taken a bite of.

Lizzie sighed. Her best friend was right, and Lizzie knew it. "I can't."

"Well, if you want, we could go halfsies on Most Photographed," Gordo offered.

Lizzie didn't even bother responding.

"Okay." Gordo shrugged and turned back to his giant map.

The bell rang, and Lizzie got up and headed toward her next class.

"You know, Lizzie," Miranda suggested as she and Gordo followed her into the hall, "you could always borrow some clothes."

"Yeah, that would be great," Lizzie said, "but stores don't lend out their clothes."

"You know," Miranda said, "I've heard of people buying their clothes for special occasions, wearing them, and then returning them and getting their money back. All you have to do is tuck a few price tags."

"And avoid all damages," Gordo pointed out.

Miranda nodded. "Oh, that's a must."

Lizzie shrugged. It was a good idea . . . but there was only one problem. "Well, I don't have enough money to buy the pants in the first place."

"Well, how much are they?" Gordo asked.

"Well, sixty-five dollars," Lizzie admitted, deciding to give up on the top, which was an extra forty-five bucks. "But I've only saved up ten."

Miranda smiled. "Well, I've got thirty dollars from my birthday," she said brightly. She stared at Gordo.

Gordo held up his hands. "Fine, fine," he said, caving in. "I've got thirty dollars, too." He cocked an eyebrow at Lizzie. "There's no downside to this investment, right?"

"No," Miranda assured him. "We buy the pants tomorrow, and we get our money back on Monday."

Lizzie winced. "But I'm supposed to go bargain hunting with my mom tomorrow."

"So, tell her we're going to study," Miranda said quickly. "Which we will. *After* we go to the mall."

Lizzie nodded, glad that Miranda had added

that they really would study. Lizzie was a horrible liar. But she could tell a half-decent half-truth sometimes.

Suddenly, Gordo jumped up next to Lizzie, smiled, then took off down the hall.

Lizzie frowned at him, but decided that it was just weird Gordo behavior—best to ignore it. She looked at Miranda hopefully. "Do you really think that this is going to work?"

Miranda nodded. "Absolutely."

Gordo trotted back, then put his hands on Lizzie's shoulder, grinned, and ducked away.

"But what if I spill something on them?" Lizzie went on.

"I'll be leading the way, keeping you out of harm's way," Miranda promised. "I'll be very poised." Miranda planted a hand on her hip.

Once again, Gordo did his dash-and-grin thing—this time, darting between Miranda and Lizzie. Okay, Lizzie thought, I can't ignore this anymore. It's getting too annoying. "Gordo, what are you doing?" she demanded, folding her arms across her chest.

"I'm just practicing my hit-and-run photo crashing," Gordo said seriously. "See, I'm going to be in all the club pictures before they even realize I'm not in their club." He waggled his eyebrows.

"I don't want to look at clothes," Matt wailed as he followed his parents around the mall. "Clothes are boring."

"Fine," Mrs. McGuire said. "I'll just be a few minutes. We can meet back at the fountain, okay?"

Matt shrugged and looked up at his dad, who nodded. "Computer games," Mr. McGuire mouthed, and Matt grinned.

Mrs. McGuire headed off in the opposite

direction. There it was—the Style Shack. "These must be the ones," she murmured, looking at the pair of ultracool hip-huggers in the window. They were denim, and frayed and studded with silver at the sides. Mrs. McGuire was sure that Lizzie would look fantastic in them. They were way beyond your ordinary jeans.

And they were way out of the McGuires' price range. Mrs. McGuire sighed and moved on. At least she knew what she was looking for now. She also knew that she and Lizzie wouldn't be able to find the exact same pair of jeans when they went bargain hunting . . . but they might be able to find something pretty similar.

Matt and Mr. McGuire stood staring at the display of games at Video Corner. There were about twenty that Matt wanted to buy . . .

especially Turbo Cops. And Ninja Meatheads. And Ultimate Grifters . . .

Suddenly, a chubby kid came up behind Matt. "It's the goofy-face kid from *The Uncle Wendell Show*!" he shouted. "Here!" the kid said, as he handed a camera to Mr. McGuire. "It works!" The kid grabbed Matt by the shoulder and grinned into his camera.

"Okay, sure," Mr. McGuire said as he squinted into the camera. "Uh. Smile."

More kids started gathering around as Matt smiled for the camera.

"Oh, yeah," Mr. McGuire said as another kid asked to have his photo taken with Matt. "Okay. Why not?"

"Hey, everybody!" the chubby kid shouted. "It's the goofy-face kid from *The Uncle Wendell Show*!"

Suddenly, a swarm of kids descended on Matt. Everyone grabbed at him, angling to get into a photo with the goofy-face kid.

"All right," Mr. McGuire said calmly. "Easy there now."

Riiiiip!

"Hey, I got a piece of the goofy-face kid's shirt!" a guy in a leather jacket shouted. Matt gaped as the kid brandished the torn sleeve in the air. The swarm of kids shouted as they lunged at Matt, looking for a souvenir of their meeting with Goofy Face.

Mr. McGuire rushed over to his son. "Come on," he shouted as he grabbed Matt's arm, "let's go!"

Matt didn't need to be told twice. He and his dad bolted through the mall . . . with the swarm of kids at their heels!

Matt and Mr. McGuire turned a corner and came face-to-face with another crowd of kids. "It's him!" one of the kids shouted.

"This way!" Matt called as he led his dad up the stairs. The kids ran after them. Matt and Mr. McGuire ran down the stairs, then up again. They hid behind a plant until the kids had passed, but more were on the way. They had to find a new hiding place! They headed for an elevator and dashed inside. Matt punched a button, and Mr. McGuire gave a little wave as the doors closed on the crowd of kids.

A few minutes later, after they'd found a suitable hideout, Matt peered down at the kids.

"Where did he go?" one of them asked. Everyone looked around, but they didn't see anything. Nothing but the tall mannequin in a long overcoat and fedora standing in the window of Lofty and Large, a shop for tall men.

"That way!" a girl shouted. The swarm followed her as she led it away.

Matt heaved a sigh of relief as he pulled off the overcoat and fedora. He had been sitting on his dad's shoulders, and Mr. McGuire helped him down. Their disguise had worked—but they had to find Mrs. McGuire and get out of the mall right away!

"There she is!" Matt shouted as he spotted his mom by the fountain. Mr. McGuire grabbed his wife, and they hightailed it out of the mall as fast as they could.

They didn't stop running until they got inside the house . . . and locked the door.

"Do you see anybody?" Matt asked. He was breathing hard.

Mr. McGuire peered out the window over the doorway. "Nope," he said as he pressed his back against the wall. "I think we lost them."

"Going through the car wash and the alley helped," Mrs. McGuire said.

Mr. McGuire nodded. "Yeah."

"Good work, Dad," Matt said as he heaved a huge sigh of relief. His father had really saved the day with some of his groupie-dodging techniques. He seemed to know something about crowd control. It wasn't that hard to picture Mr. McGuire in a dark suit and sunglasses, whispering into his lapel as he jogged next to the presidential limo. "Did you ever work for the Secret Service?" he asked his father.

"I'm not at liberty to discuss that," Mr. McGuire replied.

Matt stared at him. Well, whatever. A star could use a dad like that around.

CHAPTER FOUR

Mrs. McGuire riffled through her coupon folder while Mr. McGuire sat at the breakfast table, reading his favorite magazine—*Modern Gnome*. Everyone else in the family thought that gnomes were creepy, but Mr. McGuire was a serious collector. There were gnome lamps and lawn ornaments all over the place. "Good morning, Matt," Mr. McGuire said as his son walked into the kitchen. Mr. McGuire didn't look up from his magazine as he spoke.

"Howdy," Matt said blandly.

"What do you have planned today?" Mrs. McGuire asked.

"Right," Matt said, shaking his head. "Like I could go somewhere."

Mr. McGuire frowned, trying to remember. "Did we ground you?"

"Dad, please." Matt sighed. "I can't go out there. The people—they can't control themselves."

Mrs. McGuire pursed her lips. "So you're never going outside anymore?"

"Let's face it, Mom," Matt replied. "I'm destined to the reclusive life of a lonely, eccentric celebrity." He sighed dramatically. "Well, I'll be in my room. If you want in, knock three times fast, then yell, 'hootie-who, hootie-who,'" he said in a rather convincing owl imitation.

"If you want in *my* room, *don't* say

that," Lizzie said as she strode into the kitchen.

Mrs. McGuire grinned as she flipped though a pile of coupons. "Okay, Lizzie, it's our day to go find those clothes you want. This is going to be so much fun!"

Clearly, Mom was born to bargain hunt, Lizzie thought as she stared at her mom's eager face.

I can't lie to my mom. But I can't wear bargains.

"Ohmigosh, Mom," Lizzie said quickly. "I completely forgot—Gordo and I are going over to Miranda's house to study for a really big test." Lizzie winced. Her lies always came out sounding like—uh, lies. Still, she was pretty sure that her mom would buy this one. Mrs. McGuire didn't usually ask questions when it came to studying.

Mrs. McGuire's face fell. "Oh," she said. ". . . I thought you and I . . ."

Lizzie's heart lurched. Her mom was clearly crushed.

Mrs. McGuire squared her shoulders. "Well, that's okay," she said quickly, putting her coupons into her purse. "School comes first. I know your sizes." She smiled brightly and marched out of the kitchen.

Where is the button for lower than low? That's how i feel.

Lizzie heaved a heavy sigh. One thing's for

sure, she thought, I'm going to be the best-dressed jerk at Hillridge Junior High.

Mrs. McGuire headed straight to the outlet mall. She knew that Nell's Clothes Closet was the best place to get the really good stuff—but it wasn't going to be easy. She got there thirty minutes before the store opened, but there was already a small crowd of women waiting to get in. Mrs. McGuire took her position. She wasn't about to let these women intimidate her—not even the one who was seven feet tall and standing right behind her! Mrs. McGuire swigged some Cardio Punch and squared her shoulders.

The minute the doors opened, Mrs. McGuire dashed inside and started flipping through the clothes on the racks. There were some good things, but even at bargain prices, they were kind of expensive. Just then, a saleswoman walked over and placed a HALF OFF sign on top of the rack. Ah, bingo! Mrs. McGuire started yanking cool tops off the rack. She just knew that Lizzie would love these!

Mrs. McGuire headed over to another rack of clothes, this one filled with pants. Women were swarming around the rack, flipping through the clothes like killer ants ravaging the leaves off plants! Mrs. McGuire tried to ease her way toward the rack, but the seven-foot-woman-lady spotted her and shot her the glare of death. Okay. Mrs. McGuire knew that there must be some seriously good stuff here, so she headed to the other side, dropped to the floor, and came up on the inside of the circular rack. Now *that* was where the really good things were! She dug out a pair of black hip-huggers with silver studs down the front. Hmm . . . these had potential. They didn't look exactly like the Style Shack pants, but they were similar. Mrs. McGuire checked the price tag. $12.95. She grinned widely. "Yes," she hissed under her breath. She only wished that her daughter were here to enjoy the thrill of the bargain!

Mrs. McGuire made her way over to the cash register with an armload of cool clothes. The saleslady seemed impressed with some of her finds—and seemed even more impressed when Mrs. McGuire handed her a coupon for 20 percent off.

"You are one serious shopper," the saleslady said, shaking her head. "These clothes are great."

Mrs. McGuire grinned. "Thanks," she said. "I just hope my daughter likes them."

Meanwhile, Lizzie was doing a little shopping of her own. Miranda and Gordo had met her at the Style Shack at 11:00. By 11:01, the salesperson had pulled the famous hip-huggers—the last pair in the store—from the window display and handed them to Lizzie. Lizzie tried them on and grinned. They fit perfectly!

Two minutes later, Miranda and Gordo handed over all of their one- and five-dollar bills to the salesperson, who counted the money and put Lizzie's pants into a silver plastic bag, then smiled and handed it over to Lizzie. *Voilà!* Lizzie thought as she peeked in at her jeans one more time. Move over, cheerleaders—that award is *mine!*

The minute Lizzie got home, she rushed up to her room and pulled the Style Shack hip-huggers out of the silver bag. I swear, Lizzie thought as she gazed lovingly at the Coolest Jeans in the known universe, these pants just get better and better every time I see them. "Best Dressed, here I come," Lizzie murmured.

Someone knocked on Lizzie's door. "Just a second!" Lizzie called as she quickly dropped the pants back in the bag before shoving them under her bed. "Come in." Lizzie smoothed down her hair and sat down on her bed, as though she had just spent the last half hour sitting there casually, instead of ogling her new fashion statement.

"Look what I've got!" Lizzie's mom sang as she trotted into Lizzie's room.

Lizzie peeked into the bag. Wow. There was a lot of stuff in there—her mom had really gone crazy. Lizzie pulled out a shirt. There is something incredibly strange about this top, Lizzie thought as she gazed at the sheer ruffled blouse. The strange thing is—it's actually cool. Lizzie pulled a few more things out of the bag. Everything was awesome. Had her mom really gotten this great stuff at a bargain store?

"Oh, I have one more thing," Mrs. McGuire said giddily as she reached into another bag. "Now, I know you really wanted the pants at the Style Shack . . ." Mrs. McGuire said, waving her hand dismissively.

Ohmigosh, Lizzie thought, remembering the Style Shack bag—Lizzie would die if her mom saw the pants now. . . . She had clearly shopped like a madwoman to get Lizzie all of this great stuff.

". . . but I thought you might like these." Mrs. McGuire pulled out the pair of black jeans with a strip of metal studs down the front of each leg.

Lizzie held up the pants and caught her breath.

Wow. Not hideous. Not Style Shack. But not hideous.

"They're fantastic, Mom," Lizzie said sincerely. "And you got these on sale?"

"Honey," Mrs. McGuire said gently, "I spent less on all this stuff than I would have spent on that one pair of pants from the Style Shack."

"Oh," Lizzie said. She gave the Style Shack bag a little kick, feeling superguilty.

"Now you go out there and you win Best Dressed," Mrs. McGuire cheered.

Lizzie nodded, swallowing a lump in her throat. Mom worked her tail off to help me win, she thought. And I totally lied to her. Lizzie felt like the worst daughter in the world. But she couldn't give up now. She had the Style Shack pants . . . and she just had to win that contest. She smiled at her mom. "Yeah," she said.

I *will* win it, Lizzie told herself. I have to.

CHAPTER FIVE

Miranda checked her watch. How long had Lizzie been in there? It seemed like she should have been able to change her pants fifteen times by now.

A tall girl walked up to the girls' room door. "Oh, hey, you don't want to go in there," Miranda said, holding up her hand, traffic-cop style. "The, the toilet's overflowed," she improvised.

The girl curled her lip in disgust and headed the other way.

"Bye," Miranda called after her.

Gordo walked up and gave Miranda a little wave.

"So, how many clubs have you gotten in so far?" Miranda asked him.

"Lots." Gordo grinned. "And I just slipped into the Safety Patrol picture."

Just then, Lizzie walked out of the girls' room. She was wearing The Pants.

I think they make me look taller, Lizzie thought as she strutted out to show her friends. And they definitely make me look cooler.

"Wow!" Gordo's eyes were wide.

Miranda gaped. "Lizzie, those pants are *sweet*!"

. . . And i'd like to thank my mom and dad, and the Style Shack . . .

"Thanks," Lizzie said giddily. "Okay, are you guys ready for this day?"

"Are you kidding?" Miranda asked. "Today is our day."

Gordo nodded. "Today, we make yearbook history."

"Okay," Lizzie said confidently, and nodded. "Best Dressed." She held out her arm, and Gordo linked his through hers.

"Most Photographed," he added.

Miranda hooked her arm through Gordo's. "Most Poised."

The three friends grinned at one another and started down the hallway in perfect step. It's like we're in *The Wizard of Oz*, Lizzie thought happily. Only without the creepy flying monkeys.

But suddenly, the impossible happened. As Miranda Sanchez—serious contender for Most Poised—walked past the janitor, she tripped over his broom. She stumbled, and ran into a teacher holding a bright red Slushie.

Lizzie saw the Slushie fly into the air as though everything were happening in slow motion. Miranda fell, bringing Gordo and Lizzie down with her. "Look out!" someone yelled as Lizzie was pulled directly into the path of the oncoming Slushie, which slushed all over her Style Shack pants!

The school photographer spotted them and ran over to snap a photo of the disaster. Lizzie squinted as his flash went off—over and over and over. Now, here was a memory that would definitely be immortalized in the yearbook . . . forever.

"The pants!" Lizzie wailed. She looked down at her ruined outfit, horrified. "They're ruined!"

"I guess Most Poised is out of reach," Miranda said miserably.

Only Gordo seemed happy. "Well, at least that's one more picture I'm in!" he said.

Lizzie sighed. I'm glad one of us is having a good day, she thought.

After changing out of the Slushied pants, Lizzie walked out of the girls' room again.

"Okay, I don't even want to talk about it," Lizzie said to Gordo and Miranda. She was wearing the clothes that she had worn to school—the sheer blouse, tank top, and black, studded hip-huggers that her mom had bought. Lizzie had worn them out of the house, planning to change into the Style Shack pants at school, and then change back before she got home. That way, her mom would never know the truth. All I have to do is keep her from seeing the yearbook for the rest of my life, Lizzie thought. Of course, that little problem had taken care of itself in the form of a cherry Slushie. Now Lizzie was just glad that she had some dry, nonsticky clothes to wear. "Let's just get to class," she said unhappily.

"Okay," Miranda said as the friends started down the hall. "You know," she said, eyeing Lizzie's outfit, "I bet people still love the clothes your mom bought. Then, you can still win Best Dressed."

Lizzie rolled her eyes. "No, no. Forget about winning. What am I going to do about the pants? I can't even return them now!"

"Hey, Lizzie," Stacey Richardson said as she walked past Lizzie. "I love those pants."

Lizzie looked around and noticed that lots of kids seemed to be eyeing her jeans.

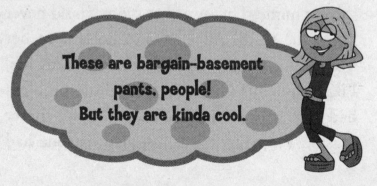

These are bargain-basement pants, people! But they are kinda cool.

"Hey, Lizzie," Ashley Cavanaugh called. "Very cool pants."

Lizzie frowned. "Thanks," she said.

Lizzie yanked open her locker and shoved the Style Shack pants inside. "I wish I had never seen these pants," she griped. "How stupid was I? I ruined a pair of pants that none of us could afford to buy, and I lied to my mom."

Gordo and Miranda looked at each other. "None of us?" they repeated in perfect stereo sound.

Grr. Lizzie pouted. Okay, so they were her pants, and she was going to have to pay Gordo and Miranda back. And I swear I will. . . . Lizzie gulped, thinking about the conversation she would need to have with her mom . . . if I live long enough.

Mrs. McGuire smiled to herself as she packed

toilet paper away into the kitchen cupboards. She loved saving money at the wholesale warehouse . . . but, she had to admit, sometimes it was tough to find a place to put all of the stuff she'd bought there.

Matt stomped into the kitchen and slapped a stack of his pictures onto the kitchen island. Mr. McGuire looked up from his paper. Matt was definitely not a happy camper.

"Matt," Mrs. McGuire said, still holding a roll of toilet paper, "what's wrong, honey?"

"What's the worst thing that could have happened?" Matt demanded.

"Are you okay?" Mrs. McGuire asked quickly. She was a mom, after all, and could think of lots of horrible things that could happen to her kids.

Just then, the doorbell rang.

"I'll get it," Mr. McGuire said as he scurried out of the kitchen.

Mrs. McGuire turned back to Matt. "Tell me," she said gently.

Matt shook his head. "Just when I was climbing the ladder of fame and fortune, I get squashed like a bug."

"What happened?" his mom asked.

"*The Uncle Wendell Show* went on hiatus," Matt said sadly, "but everyone knows that means it's canceled."

Mr. McGuire walked into the kitchen, carrying an enormous box. "I've got ten dozen 'Matt, *The Uncle Wendell Show* guy' T-shirts here," Mr. McGuire said. His eyes were huge behind his glasses. "The guy at the door says we owe him three hundred sixty dollars."

Matt's jaw dropped. "Yikes!" he shouted, scrambling out of the kitchen.

"Yeah, yikes!" Mr. McGuire called, trotting after Matt with the huge box of shirts still in his arms. "Matt!" he yelled.

Lizzie stared at her dad as he ran past her in the hall. Matt must have done something dumb as usual, Lizzie thought as she walked into the kitchen. She knew from experience that it was best to stay out of these things.

"Mom, why are you putting toilet paper in the kitchen cabinets?" she asked as she leaned against the kitchen island.

Mrs. McGuire giggled. "Well, I saved money buying the fifty-roll package," she said with a shrug. "But I ran out of places to put all of them."

Lizzie laughed, and reached for a roll. "Oh! Let me help you."

Mrs. McGuire looked at Lizzie out of the corner of her eye. "Hey, did Kate win Best Dressed?" she asked slowly.

"No."

Mrs. McGuire froze—her hand still holding a roll of toilet paper in midair—and smiled hopefully at her daughter.

Lizzie hated to shoot down her mom's dreams, but she didn't have much of a choice. "Claire did," Lizzie said. "But that's okay."

"It is?" Lizzie's mom asked.

"Yeah," Lizzie said with a smile, "because by the end of the day every girl in the school wanted to know where I had gotten my new clothes from."

Mrs. McGuire brightened. "That's great."

Lizzie shrugged. Well, it was kind of great. "But the problem is, I don't know where my new clothes came from and . . ." she struggled to find the right words. She really wanted her mom to know how grateful she was. ". . . I really wish I did, because that would have meant that I would have spent a whole, great day shopping with you. Mom, I really want you to know that I appreciate everything you did. And next time you go bargain hunting, would it be okay if I came with you?"

Mrs. McGuire smiled at her daughter. "I would love that."

Lizzie heaved a deep sigh. "Me, too," she said. And she really meant it.

A new pair of hip-huggers
from the Style Shack:
sixty-five dollars.
A more popular pair of hip-huggers
from Nell's Clothes Closet:
twelve ninety-five.
An afternoon hiding toilet paper
and laughing with my mom:
priceless.

Lizzie McGuire

PART TWO

CHAPTER ONE

Lizzie crawled down the hallway, looking like a rat. No, really. We're talking full-on rat-ness: she had on a gray headband with fake-fur ears, an itchy plastic snout with whiskers, and a rope tail. She was crawling on her hands and knees . . . and everyone was staring at her. This is so humiliating, Lizzie thought. Just then, she stuck her hand in something gooey.

Okay, now it's humiliating and *gross*, Lizzie thought. Why am I doing this again? She examined the gummy wad that was stuck to her palm. "That's disgusting!" she shouted to no one in particular. "Hello! Gum goes in trash cans, people!"

"Hey," Gordo said. He was standing at his locker, staring down at her.

"Go ahead, Gordo," Lizzie snapped, rolling her eyes. "Just say it. Just get it over with." She knew that her friend would have some smart-alecky thing to say, or possibly give her a lecture on doing things to fit in, which Gordo was heartily against. As if Lizzie hadn't been dissed enough already this morning.

"Fine," Gordo said. "Here it goes." He took a deep breath and launched into his assessment. "I think that the Diamondbacks are overrated. I mean, sure, they have the best pitching money can buy, but other than that they're a bunch of banjo-hitters and journeymen."

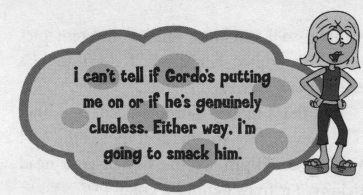

i can't tell if Gordo's putting me on or if he's genuinely clueless. Either way, i'm going to smack him.

Lizzie stood up and pointed to her rat snout. "Gordo . . ."

"Oh!" Gordo said suddenly, his eyes growing wide. "You mean about you looking like a total goober?" he guessed. "You do."

"It's for Pep Club initiation," Lizzie said, as if that were any kind of decent explanation. She pulled off the itchy rat snout. Ah, that's better, she thought.

Gordo smiled wryly. "Now, *there's* an organization worth humiliating yourself for."

"Gordo," Lizzie griped, "it's for the yearbook. I'm going to do as many activities as possible, so I can have lots of different pictures." She rolled her eyes. "I don't want a rerun of last year."

"Oh, that's right," Gordo agreed, nodding. "The only picture you made it in was the 4-H fair. You could just see the side of your head sticking out from behind a goat."

"Yeah." Ugh. Lizzie hated that picture—she would never have been caught dead at the 4-H fair in the first place if Mr. Pettus hadn't made the class attend it as part of a science requirement. "So, this year—it's a promotional blitz. I mean, the ice-cream-eating contest . . ."

Lizzie flashed back to the four-gallon tubs she had tried to scarf down in five minutes. Talk about brain-freeze!

"The Hula Club . . ." That one hadn't been so bad. The grass skirt and lei were kind of cute, actually. Unfortunately, Lizzie discovered that she didn't have much natural hula rhythm. But thankfully, you couldn't really tell that kind of thing from a yearbook photo.

"*And* the shot-put competition . . ." Okay, that club had definitely been a mistake. She'd hauled off and tried to toss the shot put as far as she could. Sadly, she forgot to let it go, and had fallen over, shot put first. She had to ice her hand for five days. Still, she was in the team photo—and that was what mattered, right?

Gordo rolled his eyes. "Who cares about being in the yearbook?" he demanded. "Talk about pointless."

Lizzie heaved a frustrated sigh. "I seem to remember that last year you tried to be Most Photographed Student, Gordo," she said, folding her arms across her chest.

"Oh, no, that was just to see if I could do it," Gordo insisted. "You know, like staying up for twenty-four hours in a row, or making the world's biggest meatball."

Or being the world's biggest meat*head*, Lizzie thought.

"And speaking of the world's biggest meatball . . ." Gordo went on. He was staring over Lizzie's shoulder.

Lizzie turned to see Kate walking toward them. She was looking even more full of herself than usual, if that were possible.

Kate sized Lizzie up and down and smiled smugly. "Oh, good, you finally found a look that works for you."

"Kate, it's for Pep Club," Lizzie said in a voice that was decidedly un-peppy. "For the yearbook."

"Oh, that's right," Kate said with a sneer. "You're in, like, eleven great pictures. You know, as editor of the yearbook, I think it's safe to say that you're in as many good pictures as anyone in school."

Lizzie grinned at Gordo.

"But since *I'm* the yearbook editor," Kate went on, "and since I have to take the pictures to the printer tonight, after Monte Carlo Nite, I'm just going to use *this* picture." Kate pulled a picture of Lizzie out of the folder she was holding and held it up. It was a giant, horrible photo. Lizzie's face was swollen and covered in blotches, and she looked like she was about to barf. "Remember that time in the cafeteria when you found out you were allergic to oyster sauce?" Kate asked perkily.

Lizzie gaped at the photo. "But . . ." she sputtered. "You . . . I . . ."

"Kate, that really isn't fair," Gordo put in.

"No, it isn't, is it?" Kate bit her lip, as though she had suddenly realized that what she was about to do was just plain evil. But then she got over it. "Oh, well!" She eyed Lizzie's rat outfit once more, and added,

"Don't go near the biology lab—they might try to experiment on you."

Even if I could think of a brilliant comeback, I'd still look like a rat searching for a contact lens.

Gordo placed the cardboard boxful of CDs he had picked up from the school music room on the DJ table. He and Lizzie were standing in the Hillridge Junior High cafeteria, and Monte Carlo Nite was being set up all around them. Everywhere, students were putting up roulette wheels, moving card tables and chairs into place, and counting chips. But even with all the excitement, Lizzie's mind was elsewhere.

"Can you believe Kate would do something so mean?" Lizzie asked.

She and Gordo exchanged a knowing glance. "Yes," they said at the same time.

Yeah, i really should have seen that one coming.

"But you shouldn't stress about it," Gordo said, still flipping through the CDs. "The more you let it bug you, the more Kate wins."

Lizzie thought about this. Gordo had a point, as usual. Kate's main purpose in life was to make Lizzie miserable, and if Lizzie took that away from her worst enemy, well, she'd have nothing left, right?

"So you're saying if I don't let it bug me, then *I* win?" Lizzie asked, just to make sure she had it right.

"Nope. Kate wins either way." Gordo responded. "So you should just forget about it and look forward to Monte Carlo Nite. You get to be the DJ. Very glamorous."

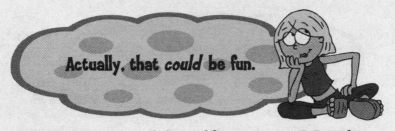

Actually, that *could* be fun.

Lizzie imagined herself as a star DJ—the crowd dancing to her funky beats as the lights strobed and the music pumped. She'd have everyone's undivided attention.

Take that, Kate!

"So, forget Kate," Gordo said, pulling Lizzie out of her reverie. "What CDs does the school have?"

Lizzie opened the box Gordo had brought

in and started flipping through the CDs. She took one out and looked at it suspiciously. *"Great Operas of 19th Century Germany,"* she said, reading the cover. They looked at one another and sneered at the school's taste in music. Lizzie picked up another CD, hoping it might be Britney or Janet. *"Sound Effects for All Occasions—Boings, Footsteps, and Steam Trains,"* she read from the next CD cover. Dare she continue down this horrible path? *"Karl Malone Reads Carl Sandburg,"* she said, shuddering. Lizzie reached for another CD. Hanson. UGH!

Gordo shook his head. He and Lizzie were clearly unimpressed with the school's taste in CDs. How would Lizzie become Hillridge's first and only superstar DJ with this selection of so-called music?

"We'll bring our own CDs from home," Gordo said.

Leave it to Gordo to come up with a quick-and-easy solution!

Just then, Kate walked by with Ethan Craft, who was Hottie of the Century according to Lizzie and almost every other girl in school. Gordo liked to think of Ethan as Dimwit of the Century, although even he had to admit that Ethan was usually a pretty nice guy.

"I thought it was Monte Carlo *Nite*," Ethan complained. "So why are we here during the day?"

Kate heaved an exasperated sigh. "I just told you—we have to find the perfect spot for the last yearbook picture—you and me enjoying Monte Carlo Nite together. After we get the perfect shot, I take the yearbook CD straight to the printer."

"Why don't we take it by the Wheel of Fortune?" Ethan suggested. "It'd be like we were on that game show." He frowned, thinking hard. "You know?" He snapped his fingers. "Oh. What's it called? It's the one with the Wheel of Fortune in it?"

Just then, Lizzie stepped in to offer her own advice. "Why don't you take the picture at the dice table, Kate? You've got snake eyes."

"Heh-heh . . . Lizzie's feisty!" Ethan said.

This is too perfect! Lizzie thought. I get to take a stab at Kate and get Ethan's attention at the same time.

"Aw, still crying over the pictures that won't be in the yearbook?" Kate bit back. "There is one open page left, and I could put you on it, or I could put me on it." She pressed her lips together, pretending to think it over. "I choose me. But I want you to know it was very close. See you tonight!" she said perkily.

Kate sauntered away, with Ethan on her arm and her nose held high in the air. Lizzie was not happy.

"There's got to be something I can do about this," Lizzie said to Gordo.

"There is. Forget about it. Who cares if you get pictures in the yearbook?" Gordo responded.

"Gordo, *you* did, last year," Lizzie reminded him.

"Well, I've grown as a person," Gordo countered. "You should, too."

"But I *want* to be in the yearbook," Lizzie said. Seriously, she thought, why isn't Gordo getting this? Is it so wrong to want to be remembered as a person who did a lot of things, instead of as a person who showed up at the 4-H fair? Was that really so shallow?

Well, okay, maybe it was shallow. But—so? The point was, Gordo was her friend, and he should be backing her up. This was something she cared about.

"Well, don't," Gordo told her. "People are

just going to look at it for two days; write, 'Have a great summer, luv ya'; and then it'll get stuck in a box with old magazines out in the garage."

Lizzie sighed. She knew that Gordo was talking from personal experience . . . *and* that he had a point. But still. It wasn't what she wanted to hear.

"And it's just pictures," Gordo went on. "What's important is that you've had the experiences that the pictures represent. Focus on that."

Lizzie bit her lip, thinking hard. Gordo was right—she had to *focus.* "I'm going to need a plan," Lizzie said. "There's got to be some way to get into the yearbook office."

Gordo shook his head in disgust. Was she listening at all? The way Lizzie's mind worked never ceased to amaze him.

CHAPTER TWO

"**H**ey, how ya doin'?" Mr. McGuire grinned suavely at Matt. "Thanks for swingin' by. You're lookin' good."

Matt stared at his father. This was definitely weird behavior—even for his dad. "Are you trying to borrow money from me, Dad?"

Mr. McGuire dug his hands into his pants pockets. "I'm practicing for Lizzie's Monte Carlo Nite. Your mom and I are on the chaperone committee for parents, and I'm assigned to be a greeter." He grinned and switched back to his supersuave voice. "Hey, let me know if you need anything. . . ." he said to an imaginary person standing nearby. "Mr. President, if you don't settle down, I'm going to have to ask you to leave," he warned. Then he cracked up and looked at Matt. "'Cause," Mr. McGuire said between giggles, "he's really very nice."

Matt had clearly had enough of this conversation. He turned to his mom. "So, what are you going to be, Mom?"

Mrs. McGuire pursed her lips. "Well, I wanted to be a blackjack dealer. You know, I put myself through grad school working on a riverboat—" She held out a deck of cards and started pouring them from one hand to another, cutting, shuffling, and flipping them at lightning speed—just like a pro! She finished by pulling the cards into a one-handed fan.

Matt stared at his mother's hands, wondering where this strange talent had come from.

Mr. McGuire looked just as shocked. "Wow."

"But, no," Mrs. McGuire griped, "they want me to be a waitress. So, I will be carrying the sodas to the card tables." She snorted in disgust. "All evening."

Matt waggled his eyebrows. "In that case, bring me an iced tea, would you, Toots?" he asked in a smooth voice. He winked at his mom. "That's my girl."

Mrs. McGuire glared at him. Matt knew that look well, and it was pretty scary.

"Or I could just get that myself," Matt said quickly.

Matt's mom gave him a tight little smile and folded her arms across her chest. "Yeah."

Matt scurried into the kitchen. He knew it was best to avoid his mother right now—she was clearly in a horrible mood over the whole Monte Carlo Nite-waitress thing.

Lizzie looked up as Matt walked into the kitchen. Perfect, she thought. Just the person I was hoping to see . . . believe it or not. "Listen, Matt," Lizzie said quickly. "I need to talk to you about something. Miranda's out of town, visiting her aunt. So—"

Matt held up his hand and blinked slowly as a smug smile appeared on his face. "Don't bother pussyfooting around, sister," he said. "You've got Kate problems, and you're look-ing for a fixer."

Lizzie gritted her teeth. Why did her annoying little brother always have the 4-1-1 on everything? "How did you know that?" she demanded.

"Trust me," Matt said smoothly. "Nothing goes on in this town that Matt McGuire doesn't sniff out." He leaned casually against the kitchen island. "So, what's your play—short grift or long con?"

Did Matt recently learn to speak Esperanto, or something? "I guess all that gobbledygook that you're talking about means you're going to help me?" Lizzie guessed.

Matt didn't reply. Instead, he just pulled a sheet of paper from his pocket, unfolded it, and slid it over to Lizzie. "My demands," he announced. "Not negotiable."

Lizzie scanned the list, and nearly choked. "Thirty-five dollars for your Christmas present?"

"Thirty-five dollars *minimum*," Matt corrected. "And it can't be anything you ever want to borrow."

Crud, Lizzie thought. Guess that cool pink sweater I'd been eyeing at the mall is out of the question. Lizzie looked back down at the list. "I don't want to do your chores for a whole month!" she griped.

Matt cocked his head. "Well, then I guess you don't want Matt McGuire," he said. "Maybe you'll get your eleven pictures in the yearbook next year."

Sometimes, with younger siblings, you just have to be patient and diplomatic. . . .

Lizzie hopped off her stool and walked over to her brother. She grabbed the waistband of his underwear and gave it a yank.

"Hey, what are you doing?" Matt cried. "No, don't do that, no! Oh, wait! Yow!"

Lizzie gave Matt a little shake.

"Okay!" Matt shouted finally. "I'll do it."

. . . But yanking their drawers up to their belly buttons can be a big time-saver!

Lizzie let go of Matt's underpants and gave him a minute to recover.

Matt took a few deep breaths, then turned his full attention to Lizzie's problem. "For this thing to work, we're going to need some help," he said. "It goes down tonight at Monte Carlo Nite, and we're going to need somebody who's just as shifty. Just as cunning . . ."

Lizzie nodded. She was pretty sure she knew where he was going, and she was with him all the way. . . .

CHAPTER THREE

Lizzie stood at the DJ table and scanned the cafeteria. She could hardly believe that she was standing in the same place that had served her rubbery fish sticks only a few hours earlier. The room had been transformed into an elegant casino. Potted palms and deep red velvet curtains lined the walls, while tuxedoed chaperones manned the gaming tables and refreshment stand.

Lizzie's eyes wandered over the room until

they landed on the target she had been searching for—the shifty, cunning linchpin in her yearbook plan . . . Matt's friend, Melina.

Melina looked over at Lizzie, who tugged at her earlobe. That was the signal asking whether all was clear. Melina tugged her ear right back indicating that the plan was still a go. Lizzie acknowledged the signal by putting her finger to the side of her nose. She couldn't help smiling—sure, Melina *looked* like a sweet, little blond girl . . . but she was as crafty as a fox, and a perfect secret weapon.

Let the games begin, Lizzie thought as she straightened her microphone headset. "Yo, yo, yo," Lizzie said in her best DJ voice, "bustin' some monsta' jamz—" Lizzie looked around the room and realized that no one could hear her. She squinted at the soundboard in front of her. Clearly, she was supposed to push or flip something. . . . There it was, a switch that toggled between BROAD-CAST and WALKIE-TALKIE. She was currently on WALKIE-TALKIE while she was communicating with Matt. So, duh, she obviously needed to switch over to BROADCAST! Lizzie flipped the switch and apologized to the crowd. "Sorry, I'm still trying to figure out this whole sound system," she admitted, her voice booming through the speakers. Then she busted out the DJ voice again. "Kick it up, big babyyy!"

Everything was good to go. Lizzie looked over to where Melina had been standing only a moment before, but she was already gone.

Let the games begin, Lizzie thought as she started the first CD. There was no stopping the plan now.

Melina hurried into a dark, deserted classroom. She flicked the lights three times, and a thick black cord dropped from the ceiling. Melina grabbed the cord and held it tight as Matt descended slowly in front of her. He was held up in a *Mission Impossible*–style black harness.

Matt whipped out a walkie-talkie and barked, "The fox is in the henhouse. The fox is in the henhouse. Phase one, complete."

Melina gave him a bored stare. "You know, I still don't see why we had to get you into the classroom this way."

Matt shrugged. "No reason. I just always wanted to do it, and it seemed like the perfect opportunity." He pressed the button on his walkie-talkie again. "Operation Lizzie's Eleven is underway. Let's roll."

Melina let go of the rope she was holding, and Matt dropped to the floor like a stone.

"I'm okay," Matt called weakly as Melina headed out the door.

"Hey, great to see ya!" Mr. McGuire said warmly to a chubby seventh grader who had just walked into the Monte Carlo Nite casino. "Thanks for coming in tonight. Glad you could come. Hey, listen, how 'bout a picture for the folks back home?" Mr. McGuire wrapped his arm around the kid, held the camera out in front of them, and snapped an instant photo. He handed the picture to the chubby kid, who was staring up at Mr. McGuire as though he were a deranged clown at a freak show. "There you go, kid."

The kid shook his head. "What a weirdo."

But despite the ratings he was getting from the guests, Mr. McGuire was having a better time than his wife. Mrs. McGuire's feet were already aching as she walked up to a gaming table and asked, "Hi, who had the ginger ale?"

"Right here, dollface," said an eighth grader sitting at the table.

Mrs. McGuire raised her eyebrows at him. "Excuse me?" she demanded. "How about *Mrs. McGuire*?"

"Ha-ha—" the kid said smarmily. "I like your sense of humor, cupcake." He dropped a blue one-dollar chip on her tray. "This is for you. Buy yourself something pretty."

Just then, the dealer behind the gaming table tried to shuffle the cards. They went everywhere—more like a game of fifty-two pickup than blackjack. "Sorry about that," the man said quickly.

Mrs. McGuire rolled her eyes. "Amateur."

Meanwhile, across the room, Lizzie walked up to Kate. She knew that she had to do this just right, or she'd never get her photos in the yearbook. It was a slim chance, but it just might work.

"I don't understand why twenty-two doesn't beat twenty-one," Ethan griped at a nearby blackjack table.

"Kate, look," Lizzie said to her ex-best friend. "I think you still have time to be fair about this whole yearbook thing."

Kate tossed her long, blond hair over one shoulder. "Why should I?" she demanded.

"Because I really, really want to be in it. I'll do anything, Kate, please," Lizzie begged. "You can borrow any of my clothes. And I'll do your homework for a whole, entire month." She smiled sweetly. "What do you say?"

Kate gave Lizzie a sunny grin. "I say, 'Go away,'" she chirped.

Just then, Gordo turned around from where he had been sitting at the blackjack table. He had clearly been winning, too, because he was holding a huge handful of chips. His nostrils flared as he scowled at Lizzie. "I'll tell you what *I* want," Gordo snapped at Lizzie. "I want you to stop making such a big deal about this stupid yearbook stuff. It's making me sick."

"Gordo," Lizzie said impatiently, "if I want to be in the yearbook, why is that any of your business?"

"It's my business because maybe I don't want to hang out with someone who gets hung up on such stupid things," Gordo shot back.

Kate raised her eyebrows. She was clearly enjoying the fact that Lizzie and her best friend were fighting. And Lizzie didn't back off. "Well, then, *don't* hang out with me," Lizzie said to Gordo.

Gordo shrugged. "Maybe I won't," he said harshly.

"Maybe you shouldn't," Lizzie agreed.

"Wow," Kate said as Lizzie and Gordo glared at each other. "I didn't mean for this whole yearbook thing to break up such a great friendship." She bit her lip and smiled. "This is such a great bonus!"

Lizzie ignored her. "Fine, Gordo," Lizzie said. "If you don't want to hang out with me, then don't. And take your stupid CDs." She grabbed a stack of jewel cases from the DJ stand—all of which Gordo had loaned her so that she wouldn't have to play German opera all night. "Here's your Celtic fusion and your South African techno-reggae and just go home," Lizzie said as she chucked the CDs at him. "Okay?"

Gordo caught the CDs . . . and dropped his pile of chips in the process. "Beats hanging around here," he said, then turned and stalked off, leaving the chips on the floor.

Kate stared after Gordo for a moment, then

looked at the floor. "Well," she said brightly, "if he doesn't want his chips . . ." Kate plopped her red-and-white, checkerboard-style handbag on the floor, then knelt down and started picking up the chips.

Spotting the chips, Melina knelt down next to Kate. "Whoa, look at all these chips!" she said. Melina put a red-and-white checkerboard-style purse down in front of Kate's. It was a dead match. But Kate wasn't paying attention—she was too busy gathering chips.

Melina leaned forward, blocking Kate's view of the purses as Matt used a long, slim hook to reach in and grab Kate's handbag. Once he had it in his hands, he walked quietly toward the exit.

Melina reached for a few chips, but Kate slapped her hand. "Hey, scram—" Kate said. "These chips are mine."

A slow smile spread across Melina's face as

she dropped the chips into the replacement red-and-white bag. "And we totally want you to get yours . . ." Melina said sweetly, holding her hands to her heart. Then she stood up and stalked off. Kate didn't ever take her eyes off the chips, and that meant so far the plan was working perfectly!

CHAPTER FOUR

Melina hurried to the stairwell, where Matt was sitting on a step, rummaging through Kate's purse. "Did you find the key yet?" Melina asked as she sat down next to him.

"No, I just started looking," Matt replied. He grimaced. "There's kind of a lot of stuff in here." He pulled an eyelash curler from the bag and stared at it suspiciously. "I think Kate tortures people," he whispered.

"Nah, that's for eyelashes," Melina told him.

Matt pulled out a wallet, three small notebooks, a pencil case, two CDs, a makeup bag, a small camera, a can of soda, and . . . a full-grown Boston terrier in a red sweater! Man, this bag was bottomless! Matt held up the dog, which yelped and trotted off, the minute Matt set it down.

"Bingo!" Matt cried as he finally pulled a small Lucite picture frame with a photo of Kate from the bag. Attached to the miniframe was a loop . . . and a key. "Got it!"

"Yes!" Melina hissed.

Matt pulled out his walkie-talkie. "This is the farmer," he said solemnly. "The goose is in the pot."

Lizzie, who was back behind the DJ table, heard Matt's voice over her headset and nodded. She flipped the switch to WALKIE-TALKIE and whispered, "Roger that, farmer. Deliver it to the kitchen. The chef is waiting." She turned the switch back to BROADCAST and shouted, "Raise the roof! Raise the *rooooof*!" The crowd on the dance floor let out a whoop. Lizzie grinned. After all, she was the one who *really* had something to cheer about.

Matt and Melina scampered to the end of the hallway. They peered around, then looked up toward the top of the stairs, where a figure was crouched in the shadows.

"'High on a hill there was a lonely goatherd—'" Melina said, using the code phrase.

The mysterious figure stepped forward. . . . It was Gordo, who brushed the side of his nose with his finger.

"The switch worked perfectly," Matt said. He grinned. "Your little fight was very convincing."

"Great," Gordo said. "Now give me the key."

"Whoa, there." Matt held up his hand and shook his head. "You got to give us the countersign first."

Gordo balked. "I am not giving the countersign. It's goofy."

"No countersign, no key," Melina said. Then she repeated the code phrase. "'High on a hill was a lonely goatherd. . . .'"

Gordo rolled his eyes. Clearly, Matt and Melina weren't giving him any choice. "Yodel-ay-hee. Yodel-ay-hee. Yodel-ay-hee-hoo," Gordo said in a bored voice.

Melina tossed him the key, giggling. Matt cracked up, too.

"That was so worth it," Melina said.

Gordo glared at her, and wondered how someone who looked so sweet and innocent could be so . . . evil.

Gordo and Melina headed into the yearbook office. It was completely dark, and they didn't dare turn on the lights. If they were caught in the office, Lizzie's eleven pictures would never make it into print.

"We're in," Gordo said into a walkie-talkie as he slid into a chair in front of a computer. He typed a few letters, and the screen flashed red.

USER PASSWORD, the computer prompted him.

"Notebook?" Gordo said to Melina, who pulled out a small pink book.

"Got it," Melina said as she handed the notebook to Gordo.

Gordo flipped through it, and frowned. "Her password is 'Beautiful Kate'?" he asked.

Melina shrugged. "She's a freak, but she's got style."

Meanwhile, Matt was back in the cafeteria—er, Monte Carlo casino. He spotted Kate dancing with Ethan near the roulette table. Suddenly, Kate's eyes narrowed, and Matt realized that Kate had noticed Larry Tudgeman, the yearbook photographer, who was there with his digital camera. Kate scurried over to Larry just as Gordo's voice came over Lizzie's headset.

"This is the chef," Gordo said. "I'm loading and formatting your pictures now. It'll take a while."

Lizzie flipped her DJ switch to WALKIE-TALKIE. "Roger that," Lizzie said. "Matt, commence 'Operation Ruin All of Kate's Pictures Until Gordo's Finished with Whatever He Needs to Do.'" Okay, so who had time to come up with fancy names for every little thing?

Matt was wearing a small earpiece. From across the room, he gave Lizzie a thumbs-up.

"Wait a minute—" Gordo complained to Lizzie through his walkie-talkie. "I had to say 'yodel-ay-hee-hoo'—that was *your* code phrase? That's bogus!"

Lizzie giggled. She had heard Gordo give the countersign over her headset and almost completely lost it when he yodeled!

"Tudgeman!" Kate shouted at Larry.

"I'm here," Larry said good-naturedly. "I'm ready!"

"Finally," Kate complained. She turned to Ethan. "Keep dancing—" she commanded. Then she looked at Larry. "It's about time," Kate went on. "I have to get this picture to the printer by midnight. Ethan!" Kate squealed. Ethan trotted over, and he posed next to Kate in front of the Wheel of Fortune. Kate rested her hand against the wheel, as though she were about to spin it.

"That's it, baby," Larry said as he peered through his camera. "You and me—making magic."

As Larry focused his camera, Matt leaned in and gave the wheel a sudden spin—and Kate, who had been leaning against it, fell backward just as Larry snapped the photo!

Lizzie saw everything and smiled. She just hoped that Gordo had enough time to load the photos and arrange them on the yearbook pages.

"Forget it!" Kate cried as Ethan tried to help her up. "Let's just take a photo near one of those palm trees."

Larry trotted after Kate as she dragged Ethan over to one of the potted trees. Kate posed at a craps table with Ethan behind her, and forced a grin for the camera. But behind her, Matt tilted the tree until the palm fronds completely covered Kate's face. Snap!

Kate frowned angrily. Another lousy photo! She looked as if she were about to strangle that palm tree.

Next, Kate and Ethan tried posing near a blackjack table. Larry looked through his lens just as Matt passed by, carrying a tray of hors d'oeuvres. Ethan stared at the food, nearly drooling. He trotted after Matt, forgetting all about the photo. Kate glared after him. It was becoming very clear that she was going to have to do this herself.

Kate walked over to the refreshment bar, which was positioned between the stereo speakers. "One mocktail, please," she ordered, shouting over the music. When the fruity drink arrived, Kate held it up and smiled for the camera.

Matt walked calmly over to the DJ stand and cranked up the volume as high as it would go. Lizzie giggled as Kate jumped about a foot in the air . . . and spilled her fruity mocktail all over Ethan. Matt nodded and turned the volume down again. Mission accomplished—for now.

But Kate was getting impatient. "I'll just take the picture myself," she snapped. "I'll get my purse, fix my makeup, and then I'll get this stupid picture taken."

Lizzie gasped. Oh, no! This could ruin everything. "Gordo, the purse!" Lizzie whispered into her headset. "She's going to figure out that we switched the purse!"

"Don't, don't worry," Gordo said as he peered at the computer monitor. "I just need, like, thirty more seconds." He turned and nodded at Melina. "And Melina's on her way with the purse."

Melina grabbed the checkered handbag and bolted out the door. This was *definitely* a job for someone crafty. And Melina *so* had it covered.

Lizzie took a deep breath and looked down

at her DJ console. She couldn't forget that she was supposed to be all over the tunes or Kate might get suspicious. Still—there was a purse to be switched.

She knew that Melina, slick as she was, couldn't handle this one alone. Lizzie flipped the BROADCAST switch and cried, "Keep dancing, everyone!" Then she checked to make sure that the next song was loaded and dashed toward the exit.

Lizzie took off down the hall and hit the bottom of the stairs just as Melina reached the second-floor landing. Wordlessly, Melina dropped Kate's purse to Lizzie, who caught it one-handed. Then Lizzie turned and leaped onto a nearby book cart. It's just like surfing, Lizzie thought as she spread her arms and rolled down the hall at top speed.

Lizzie burst through the door to the Monte Carlo casino and dove off the cart. There was no time to waste, and Lizzie burst into a series of flips across the carpeted floor. Thank you, third-grade tumbling class! Lizzie thought as she whirled over the floor. With a flying leap, Lizzie caught the edge of one of the heavy red velvet drapes, and rode it all the way over to the Wheel of Fortune, dropping Kate's real purse and using her foot to grab the phony one as she swung past.

Lizzie soared away, then let go of the drape and dismounted right behind where Matt was standing.

Mr. Lang, the journalism teacher, blinked at her, then looked away, probably just thinking he had imagined the whole thing, especially because, somehow, nobody else had seemed to notice a thing.

Kate walked over to her purse and pulled out a compact. She checked her makeup, completely oblivious to the fact that her purse had gone on a little half-hour trip.

Oh, come on, Lizzie thought as she scanned the room. Somebody *must* have seen that!

"Hey, Matt," Lizzie called to her brother, "did you see that? Did you see what I just did?"

Matt turned and frowned at her. "No, I didn't see anything."

Next time i perform, i want an announcer, a spotlight— and someone to catch me!

But Lizzie didn't have time to tell Matt about her Olympics-level tumbling routine. Kate was standing in the middle of the room— and she was posing for Larry Tudgeman!

"Kate's getting her picture!" Lizzie whispered fiercely.

Larry peered at the digital image on his camera's tiny screen. "Beautiful," he said, admiring his own work. "I used a faster shutter speed and stopped down a bit to get that whole Avedon-esque—"

"Just give me the memory card," Kate commanded, holding out her hand, palm up. "I have to load it and get it to the printer by midnight." She sneered. "I have a deadline."

Obediently, Larry handed over the memory card. "Nobody cares about art," he said with a sigh.

"Is she going to the yearbook office?" Matt asked, wide-eyed.

"Looks like it," Lizzie said, scampering over to the DJ stand. Lizzie yanked on her headset and said, "Gordo, Kate's coming! Hurry up with the yearbook!"

But, Lizzie hadn't switched the button to WALKIE-TALKIE. Her voice had just boomed out over the speakers!

Kate narrowed her eyes at Lizzie, who froze in her tracks.

"Uh . . . that was, that was . . . the song that I was going to play next, but, instead, I think I'll just play 'Mmm Bop.'" Lizzie grinned weakly. "Do you guys remember 'Mmm Bop'?"

There. That was a good cover.

"What was that supposed to mean?" Kate demanded as she stalked up to Lizzie's DJ table.

Lizzie batted her eyes innocently as "Mmm Bop" blasted through the room. "What?"

"That thing about the yearbook," Kate snarled.

Okay, keep up the act, Lizzie told herself. "When?"

Kate's teeth were clenched. "Right now. When you told Gordo to hurry up."

Lizzie pressed her lips together, then asked. "Who?"

"Fine," Kate snapped, clearly losing patience. A smile flickered at the corners of Kate's lips, and she called, "Mrs. McGuire!" Kate ran toward Lizzie's mom. It only took about three seconds for Kate to come marching back to the DJ stand with Mrs. McGuire.

"Lizzie," Mrs. McGuire said in her I-Mean-Business voice, "I want to know what's going on, and I want to know now."

"Well . . ." Lizzie hedged.

But clearly there was no way out of this one.

CHAPTER FIVE

"Okay . . . Lizzie's version of the yearbook is writing on a CD . . ." Gordo said to Melina as he stared at the computer screen. ". . . and, voilà, it is done."

"I don't think you're done quite yet," Mrs. McGuire said as she walked into the office.

"Bwaaggh!" Gordo cried, startled. He and Melina turned to see Mrs. McGuire. She was frowning. Behind her, Kate was grinning, and Lizzie was looking worried.

"Uh. I'm going to get a drink of water," Melina said quickly. "At my house," she added, backing toward the door. "We have a filter." Lizzie stared after her as Melina hurried out the door.

"You know," Gordo said to Mrs. McGuire, "you're looking quite ravishing this evening."

Mrs. McGuire lifted her eyebrows at him. "And you're looking very guilty." She pointed to the CD, which was now loaded with Lizzie's eleven yearbook pictures. "What have you got there?"

Gordo grabbed the CD. "Oh . . ." he said slowly, ". . . nothing."

"That's the yearbook CD," Kate spat out. "It's mine, and I want it right now."

"Gordo . . ." Mrs. McGuire commanded, looking from him to Kate.

Reluctantly, Gordo handed the disc to Kate. Kate yanked the disc with Lizzie's photos out of the CD drive and put her own disc in. "See, Mrs. McGuire?" Kate said, holding up Lizzie's disc. "This is the disc they thought they could switch for mine."

Mrs. McGuire held out her hand. "Give it here." She nodded at the computer. "Load in your picture."

Kate flipped her hair over one shoulder and sneered at Gordo. "Do you mind?" she asked. Gordo leaped out of his seat while Kate loaded her new photo onto the disc.

"You know," Gordo said to Mrs. McGuire, "you really should wear your hair like that every day."

Mrs. McGuire didn't even look at him. "Put a sock in it, Gordo."

Gordo nodded. "You betcha."

Kate peered at the computer screen and smiled triumphantly. "There," she said. "My Monte Carlo picture is loaded and in place."

She flashed Lizzie a smug little smile. "Isn't it pretty, Lizzie?" She gloated.

Lizzie made a face, but Kate just ignored her and pressed SAVE. "There," Kate said. "Done."

Mrs. McGuire pressed the button on the CD drive, and the tray slid out. She pulled out the disc and handed it to Kate. "Okay," Lizzie's mom said. "Take this directly to the printer."

"I'm on my way," Kate said in her perkiest voice. She headed toward the door, then paused. "Oh, thanks, Mrs. McGuire," she said with forced kindness. "You've really helped to make the yearbook just right." Then she smirked at Lizzie and flounced out.

Lizzie watched her go. She just couldn't believe this was happening. . . . Lizzie turned to her mom.

"Lizzie," Mrs. McGuire said, "Gordo . . ." She shook her head. "You guys were very convincing." A grin broke over her face.

Gordo gave her a double thumbs-up.

I just can't believe this actually worked! Lizzie thought. "You were even better!" Lizzie gushed to her mom. "She totally believed every word that you said!"

Just then, Mr. McGuire walked into the room, followed by Matt.

"Hey, how ya' doing?" Mr. McGuire greeted everyone with a broad smile. "Everybody having a good time?"

"Well, did it work?" Matt asked eagerly.

"Every step of the way," Lizzie told him. "Kate totally believed that Gordo was mad at me, so she went for the spilled poker chips just like we knew she would—" Lizzie nearly laughed out loud as she remembered Matt and Melina grabbing the purse as Kate dove for the poker chips like they were solid-gold Mardi Gras beads.

"Well, you did your little 'broadcast switch' mix-up just right," Matt told Lizzie. "I didn't think you could pull it off."

Mr. McGuire looked at Lizzie. "And why did Kate have to think she'd busted you?"

"Well," Lizzie explained, "because we knew that she'd put her pictures on her yearbook CD." Lizzie knew that having her *own* eleven pictures stored on a CD didn't mean anything unless she had some way to get that disc to the printer. She also knew that once Kate had at last taken her final yearbook photo, she would head straight to the yearbook office to load it. By exposing Matt's plan over the loud-speaker and "getting busted" by Kate, Lizzie was given the opportunity to switch the two discs—and pass her own disc, with all her eleven pictures, to the printer! Actually, Lizzie thought, it was Mom who did all the work when it came to the switching...

"And it got me into the room to switch the discs, so I ended up giving Kate Lizzie's CD," Mrs. McGuire said as she thought back to how she used her expert card-shuffling skills to swap the two discs right inside the drive before she passed Lizzie's disc off to Kate.

Lizzie nodded. She had to admit, her mom had been amazing with the sleight of hand. Even Lizzie hadn't noticed when Mrs. McGuire switched Kate's disc with her own.

Mrs. McGuire shrugged. "So I guess that my cardsharp skills got used at least one time tonight."

Matt waggled his eyebrows. "I can think of a million ways to use them."

Mrs. McGuire planted her hands on her hips. "No, no, no," she insisted. "Kate went over the line with the yearbook—so this was a *one-time* deal."

"Your mother only uses her grifting skills for good," Mr. McGuire said, "not evil."

i never thought about it, but parents have to be con artists. How else would they get us to eat our vegetables, or go to bed on time, or send thank-you notes for crummy presents we've already exchanged for store credit?

Just then, Melina poked her head into the yearbook office. "You know," she said, "there hasn't been any music playing for, like, what? Ten minutes?"

Lizzie's eyes grew wide. "Whoa!" she cried as she hurried out the door.

Mrs. McGuire laughed as she watched her daughter leave. Melina looked at Mrs. McGuire. "And they're complaining about not getting their drinks," Melina went on.

Mrs. McGuire winced and hurried toward the door. "Oops!"

"Ohmigosh!" Mr. McGuire said suddenly. "There's nobody in there greeting them!"

"They said they're glad you're not hassling them anymore," Melina told him.

Matt laughed, and his dad gave him a playful swat on the head. "Ow!" Matt complained.

Hey—the truth hurts.

Lizzie scampered back to the DJ table and put on a dance record. No more Hanson. *"Très bien, mes amis!"* Lizzie said into her microphone. "That's 'Okay, everybody' in French—" she explained. "Monte Carlo Nite is almost over. So, one more song, and it's *au revoir*."

Lizzie grinned. "That's French for 'we're outie.'" Lizzie turned up the volume on the song and stood back, watching the people dance.

"Well, however you say it," Melina told Lizzie, "you got your pictures in the year-book."

"Yeah," Lizzie said. "But you know what the best part was? It was all of us doing it together. I mean, coming up with the plan, and each of us doing our own thing. That was really cool."

it's true. i mean, pictures fade, and they get torn, and stuff spills on them, and your haircut looks really dorky, but memories last forever.

Lizzie looked across the room, where her parents were standing together by the bar. They touched their noses at her, giving her "the signal." Lizzie, Gordo, Matt, and Melina brushed their noses in reply.

Mission accomplished, Lizzie thought happily. She couldn't wait to see the yearbook. But it wasn't just because she'd have eleven great photos inside. As Gordo had said, what's important are the experiences that the pictures represent. And Lizzie knew that—even if her yearbook did end up buried somewhere in the back of the garage—she would never, ever forget tonight.

Don't close the book on Lizzie yet!
Here's a sneak peek at the next
Lizzie McGuire story. . . .

Adapted by Jasmine Jones
Based on the series created by Terri Minsky
Based on a teleplay written by Melissa Gould

"**N**o, no, no," Lizzie said as her best friend, Miranda Sanchez, danced to the pop music that was blasting from the CD player. When Lizzie and Miranda's other best friend, David "Gordo" Gordon, had announced that he wanted to shoot a music video, the girls had jumped at the chance to dance in it. They'd been working on their choreography for the past three days, and it was really starting to come together. Lizzie swung her right arm across her body with staccato rhythm—"It's Britney, Britney, Janet," Lizzie demonstrated. Then she did a funky head move—"And then J.Lo."

Miranda shook her head. "Wrong," she replied, then busted into her own order of the dance moves. "It's Britney, *Janet*, Janet—"

"I'm hearing music . . ." Gordo said as he walked into Lizzie's living room with a tray full of snacks.

He really has an unnatural ability to sniff out junk food in my family's kitchen, Lizzie thought as she eyed the munchies. I mean, where did those Cheese Puffs come from?

"I'm seeing dancers . . . getting a whiff of that sweet smell of success," Gordo continued as he plopped the tray onto the coffee table.

"I need to refuel," Miranda said, diving toward the snacks. She shoved a chocolate chip cookie into her mouth, and Gordo flopped down on the couch.

"Me, too," Lizzie agreed, lunging at the Cheese Puffs. Then her eye fell on something even better. "Peanut butter!" she cried, grabbing the jar and a soup spoon.

Miranda wolfed down another cookie as Lizzie licked her spoonful of peanut butter. Yum!

Gordo shook his head as he watched the girls scarf down the goodies. "Man, you guys eat *a lot*!" He took a bite of a Cheese Puff.

Lizzie ignored him. "Ooh, I should get some pretzels!" she said to Miranda. Lizzie thought that pretzels dipped in peanut butter were deelish!

"You guys think you could stop stuffing

your faces long enough for us to finish rehearsal?" Gordo asked.

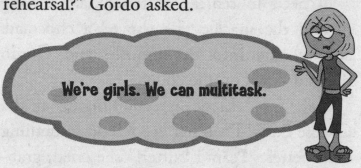

We're girls. We can multitask.

"Gordo, just 'cause we're eating doesn't mean we're not rehearsing," Miranda said through a mouthful of chocolate chip cookie.

Lizzie nodded in agreement, tossing her long blond hair over her shoulder. She and Miranda had been dancing for two hours straight! Who cared about a spoonful-of-peanut-butter break?

"You guys, this music video needs to be taken seriously." Gordo leaned forward on the couch to drive his point home. "I'm branching out. Expanding my repertoire."

"Yeah, it'll look good on your school record," Miranda agreed, sending cookie crumbs flying. She pointed to herself and turned to Lizzie. "Ours, too, Lizzie."

Okay, Gordo's making sense, but Miranda?

Lizzie raised her eyebrows. Since when did Miranda worry about school records? She was just about to ask Miranda what she was talking about when Lizzie's annoying little brother, Matt, walked into the living room with his best friend, Lanny. The good thing about Lanny, as far as Lizzie was concerned, was that he never said a word. This was more than she could say for her little brother, who unfortunately always seemed to have something weird to share. Like right now, for example. He was standing there in a black turtleneck and a goofy-looking beret, staring at Lizzie, and she just knew that he was going to say something irritating. It was only a matter of time. He gaped at her, and held up his finger and thumb in an L shape, as though he were framing her face with his hand. Lanny held up his thumb and nodded.

Lizzie narrowed her eyes at Matt. "What are you staring at?"

"Watch a *real* artist at work," Matt said in a bored voice. He lowered his eyelids and smirked at her, then took a massive sketch pad from Lanny and began to scribble away on it like a madman.

"Whatever you're doing, stop!" Lizzie commanded, folding her arms across her chest.

But Matt didn't listen . . . as usual. His

hand just kept flying across the page. Finally, he looked up at his sister and flipped his sketch pad over. "Behold," he said, holding up a charcoal drawing of Lizzie.

The picture on his pad actually kind of looked like Lizzie—sort of. That is, it looked like Lizzie if her mother had been a rectangle and her father a trapezoid. The drawing was abstract . . . but you could still make out the resemblance. "I call this one 'Girl Who Makes Me Hurl,'" Matt said in a haughty voice.

Lizzie planted her hands on her hips. "Well, I call this one 'Brother About to Run for His Life.'"

Matt scrambled out of the room, and Lizzie dashed after him.

Miranda frowned and then called out to Lizzie, "Could you get those pretzels while you're up?"

Sorry! That's the end of the sneak peek for now. But don't go nuclear! To read the rest, all you have to do is look for the next title in the Lizzie McGuire series—

GET INSIDE HER HEAD

Lizzie McGuire

A Disney Channel Original Series

Weekends
Watch it on

Visit Lizzie every day at DisneyChannel.com